This rising moon book belongs to:

_____

DATE DUE

SEP 1 0 2002		
OCT 08 2002		
DEC 1 0 2002		
DEC 3 0 2002		
JAN 0 7 2004		
NOV 0 2 2004		

CLEAR MOON, SNOW SOON

TONY JOHNSTON

illustrated by GUY PORFIRIO

rising moon

www.northlandpub.com

The illustrations were rendered in oils
The text type was set in Janson MT
The display type was set in Garamond
Composed in the United States of America
Designed by Lois A. Rainwater
Edited by Aimee Jackson

Printed in Hong Kong

10 9 8 7 6 5 4 3 2 1

FIRST IMPRESSION
ISBN 0-87358-785-5

Johnston, Tony, date.
Clear moon, snow soon / Tony Johnston ; illustrated by Guy Porfirio.
p. cm.
Summary: A child anticipates the arrival of an old man in red, smelling of pine, spreading crinkling presents late at night.
ISBN 0-87358-785-5
[1. Santa Claus—Fiction. 2. Christmas—Fiction.] I. Porfirio, Guy, ill. II. Title.

PZ7.J6478 Cl 2001
[E]—dc21   2001019108

For Aimee Jackson

—T. J.

To Katherine, my little princess

—G. P.

Clear moon, snow soon.
An old man in red will come to visit
when I'm in bed.

And he'll smell of pine.
And peppermint.
And maybe gingerbread.

He'll hum. But no one will hear the tune of his old, old song, except the moon.

He'll dance. But no one will hear the tread of his sooty boots. He'll dance barefoot!

No one at all will see him spread
crinkling presents in the hall.
No one at all except the doll.

I won't sleep a wink.

I'll listen for the shake
of bells on a sleigh.
Bells that say he's come.

Then I'll sneak from bed.

thank you
for the cookies
my dears
love Santa

Down the stairs I'll creep.

And still as snow or moon,
I'll peek at an old man in red.

One Christmas TONY JOHNSTON came upon an old cross-stitched pillow in a shop. It showed a scene of the moon hung among tall pines and said, "Clear Moon, Snow Soon." She bought the pillow for her agent, Susan Cohen, then wrote a story—*Clear Moon, Snow Soon*.

Mrs. Johnston has published more than a hundred books for young readers, and has won numerous awards and honors for her work. She lives in California.

A native of Chicago, GUY PORFIRIO graduated from the American Academy of Art in Chicago, and continued his training at the New York School of Visual Arts. He has received numerous awards and honors for his work over the years. Though Guy now lives in Tucson, Arizona, he has never forgotten the joy and wonder of Christmas that he felt as a child growing up in snowy Chicago. *Clear Moon, Snow Soon* is his third children's book.